# THE USBORNE BOOK OF
# BEDTIME STORIES

## Written and retold by Philip Hawthorn

## Illustrated by Stephen Cartwright

Designed by Amanda Barlow

Edited by Jenny Tyler

Cover Design by Non Taylor

With thanks to Ray Gibson, Ronald Lloyd and Christopher Rawson

This edition first published in 2000 by Usborne Publishing Ltd,
Usborne House, 83-85 Saffron Hill, London EC1N 8RT

Printed in Great Britain

# Contents

There are little yellow ducks hidden in this book. How many can you find?

# THE LITTLE RED HEN

In a small cottage there lived a pig, a cat, a duck and a little red hen. The little red hen was a busy red hen who spent all day cleaning the house, polishing the windows and digging the garden. The other three animals were incredibly lazy, and never did any work at all.

One day, the little red hen found a grain of corn. "Who will help me plant this grain of corn?" she asked.

"Not I," said the pig, with a grunt and a sigh.

"Not I," purred the cat, lying down on the mat.

"Not I," said the duck on the pond, with a "quack".

So the little red hen planted the grain of corn all by herself.

All through the spring and summer the grain grew and grew until it ripened into a tall, golden ear of corn. Then the little red hen knew that it was harvest time.

"Who will help me harvest the corn?" she asked.
"Not I," grunted Pig, with the laziest sigh.
"Not I," purred the cat, from her comfortable mat.
"Not I," said the duck, with a splash and a "quack".

So the little red hen harvested the corn all by herself, pecking at the stalk until it fell over. Then she separated the grains from the husks and carefully placed them in a handkerchief - all except for four, which she saved in a drawer.

"Who will help me take the corn to be ground into flour?" she then asked.

"Not I," said the pig from his mud, with a sigh.

"Not I," purred the cat, all curled up on the mat.

"Not I," said the duck, swimming by with a "quack".

So the little red hen took the grains of corn to the miller all by herself, and asked him to grind them into flour.

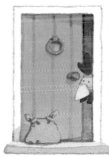

After a few days, a small bag of flour was
delivered to the cottage where the animals lived.

"Oh good," said the little red hen. Then she
shouted, "Who will help me make the flour into
bread?"

"Not I," said the pig. "I'm asleep in my sty."

"Not I," purred the cat. "I'm asleep on my mat."

"Not I," said the duck with an extra loud "quack".

"All right," sighed the little red hen. "I shall have
to make it all by myself." She went into the
kitchen, tipped the flour on to the table, added
some water and yeast, then kneaded the mixture
into a dough. When the dough had risen, she
popped it into the oven to bake.

Soon the smell of fresh bread wafted through the
house, into the garden, and even to the pond.

When it reached the pig, he wrinkled his snout and
all of a sudden felt very hungry. So he heaved himself
out of the mud, and trotted into the house. Behind
him was the cat, and behind her was the duck.

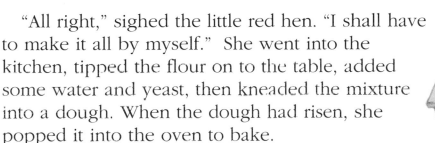

They arrived in the kitchen just in time to see the little red hen open the oven door. Inside was the tastiest looking loaf of bread that any of them had ever seen.

"Now, who is going to help me eat my bread?" asked the little red hen.

"Me!" said the pig, fairly grunting with glee.

"And me!" purred the cat. "It's time for my tea."

"And me!" said the duck with a waddle and "quack".

"Tough luck!" replied the hen. "All this work has made me so hungry that I'm going to eat it all myself. But I'll tell you how you *can* get some bread."

"How?" they said, eagerly. And the little red hen took out from the drawer three of the four grains of corn she had saved, and gave one to each of the other animals.

"Get planting!" said the hen. The pig, the cat and the duck went out to plant their grains. "I'll plant mine when I've eaten," thought the hen. Then she sat and ate her bread - every last crumb.

# BUTTON NOSE

 An old woman was sitting in her chair by a cosy evening fire. She was just dozing off, when the door burst open and in rushed her granddaughter.

"Hello Grandma!" yelled the girl. Then she ran excitedly over to the old woman and gave her a big hug.

"How was your holiday?" asked the old woman.

"Great, thanks. We went to a place called Lillia, and do you know what? On the day we left everyone was walking around with their fingers ..."

"Pressing their noses flat, like buttons?" the old woman said, finishing the sentence.

"Yes!" said the girl. "How did you know?"

The old woman sighed. The glow from the fire was just bright enough to show the sparkle in her eyes as she told her granddaughter this story ...

Long ago in the land of Lillia there was a poor peasant and his wife. When they had been married for only a year, she had a son. He was a pretty child, but as he was growing up, his parents realized that there was one part of him that wasn't growing: his nose. It remained small, round and pink - just like a button. The other children would run after him calling, "Button Nose, Button Nose!" This made him sad, because he longed to be friends with the children and join in their games.

One day, when Button Nose was quite big (except for his nose, of course), a dreadful thing happened. A nasty witch called Witch Hazel cast a spell on the King and Queen of Lillia, banishing them to the top of a glass tower. No-one was able to rescue them because the tower was impossible to climb.

Witch Hazel became the ruler of Lillia, and everyone was afraid. From that moment no birds sang, the flowers all died, and everyone spoke in whispers and never smiled. Poor Button Nose worked in the palace, doing all the nasty jobs such as chasing rats from the kitchen, fetching wood from the cellar and cleaning the toilets.

One evening, Button Nose heard a great howling and wailing coming from the dining hall. He went to investigate, and found that the noise was being made by the witch who was singing. As it was her birthday, she was celebrating, and had drunk three bottles of wine. Feeling nervous and swallowing hard, Button Nose wished the witch a happy birthday.

"You're rrrright!" croaked the witch. "It is happy. I am the queen of all the land, and no-one can take that away from me."

Button Nose suddenly felt brave, and said, "You must be very clever Queen Witch Hazel, because no one can find a way to break your spell and free the old king and queen."

"Of course not. How could they know that the only way to break it is to show me something that no one has ever seen before?" replied the witch. "Even if they did know, they'd never find anything because as soon as they found it, they would see it - so when *I* saw it, it would have been seen before ... see?" The witch cackled and began to sing again. It was so loud that the windows rattled and the cat darted under the stairs and put its paws over its ears.

Poor Button Nose spent a restless night. If only he could think of something that no one had ever seen before.

Next day, he told the witch there were some people outside with presents for her. In spite of a bad headache, she became very excited, and put on a large ruby crown that she'd found in the jewel cupboard.

"Summon the peasant present bearers!" she said, in as regal a voice as she could manage.

The door opened and in came the royal gamekeeper, carrying a silver plate on which was a magnificent fish. Its scales shimmered red, then blue, then green - and its tail was silver, like moonshine.

Button Nose, his knees knocking, said, "I bet no one has ever seen the like of this before."

"Don't be silly," said the witch sharply. "The old fool saw it himself when he caught it." Then she turned on Button Nose. "And talking of being caught, were you hoping I'd be caught out by your sneaky trick?"

"Er, no, your majesty, whatever gave you that idea?" he said, trying not to go red. Then thinking quickly he added, "I have a present for you, too."

"Oh?" said the witch, raising an eyebrow.

"Your Majesty, I would like to give you this!" And Button Nose produced a plate on which was a shiny green apple and a knife.

"An apple?" shouted the witch. "What sort of present is that for a Royal Person such as me?"

"Just have a look inside, your Highness," begged Button Nose. "Then you'll get a big surprise."

Witch Hazel sat down. She thought that there might be a jewel hidden in the apple, so she snatched up the knife, sliced the apple down the middle and peered at the two halves.

"Why, you little beast, there's nothing here!" said the witch.

In a flash there was nothing of her either. She vanished in a puff of smoke, and in her place sat the king and queen. Button Nose's trick had worked, and the magic spell had been broken, because the witch had looked at the inside of the apple, which no one had ever seen before.

The king and queen were so grateful to Button Nose that they promoted him to head butler. In his honour they decreed that every year, on his birthday, everyone should keep their noses pressed flat - as flat as a button.

# NAIL SOUP

One winter evening, just as the sun was going down, a tramp knocked at the door of a cottage and asked for shelter.

"Oh, all right," grumbled the old woman who lived in the cottage. "Don't expect any food, though, because my cupboard's as bare as a baby's bottom."

The tramp sat by the meagre fire feeling cold and hungry. Then he had an idea. Smiling, he took an old nail from his pocket.

"This here's a magic nail," he said. "Last night it made the best nail soup I have ever tasted."

"Nail soup? I've never heard anything so stupid in all my born days," said the woman with a scowl.

"It's true," the tramp continued. "All I did was to boil it in a saucepan. Do you want to try some?"

Although the old woman was far from convinced, she decided she would play along. "Go on then," she said. "But you'll have to show me how to do it."

"Right. First we need a cooking pot half full of water," said the tramp. The old woman fetched one, and the tramp put it on the stove. Then he dropped in the nail and said,

"Nail we trust that all your rust,
Will make a tasty soup for us."

Then he sat down and waited. After a while the woman became curious and peeped into the pot.

"Last night I added some salt and pepper. It made an ordinary soup into a good soup," said the tramp.

So the old woman went to her cupboard, fetched the salt and pepper and put some into the water.

After a few more minutes, she looked into the pot again.

"Pity you haven't any food," said the tramp stroking his chin. "A single onion would make a good soup very good."

"I'm sure I could find one," said the woman, her curiosity growing stronger. She went and looked in her larder. As she opened the door, the tramp saw that inside the shelves were groaning under the weight of all kinds of food.

"Why, you mean old thing," said the tramp to himself.

He stood for a while, silently stirring the onion into the soup. Then he said, "Shame you haven't got any carrots and potatoes to go with the onion, or a parsnip. They would make a very good soup extremely good."

The woman was now feeling pretty peckish, and she disappeared again into the larder. She emerged with an armful of fresh vegetables, which she peeled and chopped. The tramp put them into the pot.

"This is coming along nicely," said the tramp. "But I tell you what."

"What?" said the woman, her tummy rumbling like distant thunder.

"Some tender, lean meat would make an extremely good soup amazingly good." The woman fairly ran to the larder and came back with a huge piece of steak which she cut up and gave to the tramp to pop into the pot.

By now, the soup was beginning to smell delicious. The tramp said, "Pity to have to eat such an amazingly good soup at such a boringly bare table. I always think food tastes better when a table is properly laid, don't you?"

"Of course," said the woman. Not wanting to spoil the soup, she fetched her best tablecloth and spread it on the table. Then she got out china soup bowls and

shiny silver spoons, and even some candlesticks with candles in them.

The tramp stirred the soup for a bit longer, then he said. "Shame you have no food in the house, because some bread would make an amazingly good soup, simply soooper." Again the woman ran to the larder, this time fetching a loaf of bread that she had baked that morning.

Finally, the tramp sighed and shook his head.

"What's the matter?" said the woman, her mouth watering at the smell of the soup.

"I was just thinking that it's such a great pity we can't have any wine with the soup. You see, wine would make a - "

But the woman wasn't listening. "I'm sure I've got some somewhere," she said, rushing into her cellar. She brought back a fine-looking old bottle and two of her best glasses.

"Now, I think the soup is just about ready," said the tramp, carefully removing the nail and putting it back in his pocket. Then they sat down at the table and had an absolute feast.

After she had finished, the old woman declared it was the best soup she had ever tasted. Then she offered the tramp cheese, apple pie and chocolates to thank him, all of which they washed down with another bottle of wine.

Then they told each other stories and jokes until the candles had burnt themselves out.

The old woman gave the tramp her bed to sleep in, while she dozed off in her chair.

And there are no prizes for guessing what they dreamed about: the simply soooper nail soup.

# DRAGON TRAIN

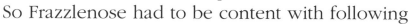

Once there was a town called Wibblington. Next to this town was a mountain, and on this mountain lived a friendly dragon called Frazzlenose, who loved steam trains. It might have been because they puffed out smoke rather like he did; or because they carried lots of his favourite food, coal. The fact remained that he was never happier than when he was flying along next to a train - especially, the Wibblington Express.

The trouble was, the people on the train didn't know that Frazzlenose was a kind dragon. Every time he appeared they screamed, "It's a dragon! Quick, hide! He'll sizzle us to a crisp with his breath!"

So Frazzlenose had to be content with following

the train from high up in the sky, out of sight of the
nervous passengers.

Wibblington was in a large country, governed by a
large queen called Good Queen Daisy. It was her
custom, every New Year's Day, to choose a town in
her queendom for a special royal visit. The town
would then be known as The Royal Town for the
whole year, and receive a gold statue of the queen. It
was the greatest honour a town could wish for.

One day, whilst the people of Wibblington were
going about their normal business, a messenger
galloped into the market square on his horse.

"Hear ye! Hear ye!" he proclaimed in a loud voice to the people, who were quickly gathering round. "Know ye that Her Royal Highness Good Queen Daisy has elected the humble town of Wibblington for the most splendiferous honour that any town ..."

"Get to the point, will you!" interrupted a man.

"Yes, it's freezing standing around here!" said a woman. The crowd grumbled in agreement.

The messenger sighed, put down his scroll, and said, "You're going to be the next Royal Town."

"Hooray! Hoorah! Hoo-wibble!" shouted the people. Then they pulled the man from his horse and gave him a plateful of peanut butter sandwiches and a huge mug of tea. The horse got a bucket of oats.

"The queen will arrive on New Year's Day to make the official announcement," said the messenger between mouthfuls. Then he finished his tea with a big slurp, climbed on to his horse and rode back down the road, hiccupping loudly as he went.

During the next few days the people were very busy. The town was tidied, swept, cleaned, scrubbed and polished ready for the royal visit. Pillar boxes

gleamed, lamp posts sparkled, and you could see your face in the cobblestones. The train was also cleaned, for on the morning of New Year's Day it would leave to pick up the queen from her palace.

At last, New Year's Day arrived. The train was given a last-minute polish, and the red carpet was laid out ready for when it returned carrying the Most Important Person. The people scrambled on board, and were so excited that they didn't really notice the snow that was beginning to fall. The Wibblington Express puffed out of the station and began the journey to the palace. Frazzlenose followed at a safe distance. The snow continued to fall.

By the time the train reached the palace, the snow was almost as high as the funnel. The queen's royal coach was joined on to the rest of the train, and all was ready for the return journey. But despite a lot of huffing and puffing, and a good bit of chuffing, the train stayed absolutely still. It was stuck in the snow.

"Oh dear," said the queen. "What a to-do. I can't possibly get to Wibblington today. I shall have to find another, nearer town. I'm very sorry."

The people were overcome with disappointment. Some of them shed tears, others just looked out of the window at the still-falling snow, thinking that it was unlikely they would be chosen again. Even the train looked sad.

Suddenly, from the grey, snowy clouds came a whooshing of wings and a crackle of fiery breath. "It's the dragon!" they shouted. "As if things weren't bad enough, now he's come to finish us off." They put their hands over their heads and prepared to be burnt to a cinder.

The next thing they knew, the train was moving.

They looked out of the windows and saw
something quite astonishing. Sitting on the front of
the train, breathing all the fire he could muster, was
Frazzlenose. As he breathed, the snow on the railway
tracks melted, and the train was slowly able to head
for home.

The people cheered with all their voices, "Three
cheers for ... what's the dragon's name?"

"Frazzlenose," shouted Frazzlenose, between hot
snorts.

"Three cheers for Frazzlenose! Hip-hip hoo-
wibble!" they chorused. Even the queen joined in.

The train got back to Wibblington and the
celebrations began. Good Queen Daisy made a
speech, they all ate the biggest banquet the town had
ever produced - and who do you think was guest of
honour?

Frazzlenose, of course. He sat at the queen's table,
wearing the train driver's hat and crunching away at
his plate of coal.

After that, Frazzlenose was allowed to travel on the
train whenever he wanted to. He was even allowed
into the cab, provided he promised not to eat all the
coal. He was very useful when the engine needed an
extra blast of fire on really steep hills.

When the gold statue arrived from the queen, on it
were written the words:

"To The Royal Town of Wibblington
and its Dragon Train."

# THE PRINCESS AND THE PEA

 Long ago, there was a land where the mountains were capped with snow, the pastures were rich and green and the people were happy. In this land there lived a prince who was so handsome, so friendly and so kind that every girl in the land fell in love with him. But the prince was so fussy that he only wanted to marry a princess, a real princess.

He travelled far and wide looking for his ideal princess, but there was always something wrong. Either they were too tall for him, or too short, or they were too grumpy and never smiled. After many months of searching, the prince came home and said to the king and queen, "It's no good, I can't find a princess I like enough to marry. I shall have to live alone to the end of my days."

A week later, the royal palace was in the grip of a ferocious blizzard. Snow beat against the windows and whistled into every crack it could find. In the middle of the night there came a timid knock at the door.

The king got out of bed. "Who can that be on a night like this?" he asked. He went downstairs and shuffled across the hall. Yawning, he opened the door a little, and in the light that spilled out into the night, he saw a girl. She was shivering with cold and half covered in snow.

"You poor dear," said the king. "Come on in and warm yourself by the fire."

"Th-th-thank you," said the girl, hardly able to keep her teeth from chattering. She went and sat by the palace fire, whilst the king warmed up some milk for her. By this time the queen and the prince had also joined them.

"I was looking for the palace, but it was much further than I thought," said the girl, whom the prince thought quite pretty. "You see, I'm a princess." The prince's eyes widened, and his heart beat faster.

The queen knew exactly what her son was thinking, but she thought the girl was probably only pretending to be a princess. She asked her to stay the night so that she could set a trap for her.

While the girl was having a good splash in a hot bath, the queen went to prepare her bedroom. First she placed a dried pea under the mattress of the bed. Then she sent two maids to all the other bedrooms in the palace to find extra mattresses and eiderdowns. Altogether they collected twenty of each. They piled them up on top of each other: first the mattresses, then the eiderdowns - until they almost reached the ceiling.

When the girl was ready for bed, she had to climb a long ladder to get into it.

"Nightie-night," said the queen. Then she added in a low voice, "In the morning we shall know whether or not you are a real princess."

Next morning at breakfast, the queen asked the girl if she had slept well.

"You have been very kind to me," she replied, a little uneasily. "I don't want to sound ungrateful, but I couldn't sleep a wink because I could feel something small and hard in my bed." Seeing the king, the queen and the prince smiling broadly at each other, the girl added crossly, "Well I don't know why you're all so happy - I'm as bruised as an old apple now."

"We're smiling because in order to feel something as small as a pea through all those soft layers you must be a real princess," said the prince. "Err ... will you marry me?"

The girl's frown turned into a huge grin, and she threw herself into the prince's arms.

The prince and princess lived happily together for many years. They had seven children, who were all given names that began with a "P", because that's how their love had begun - with a pea.

# THE SQUIRE'S BRIDE

 There was once an old squire who was very rich. His pockets bulged with his money, and his waistcoat bulged with his fat, overfed stomach. He lived in a huge house, and owned all the land as far as the eye could see. He had everything a man might want; everything, that is, except a wife. So he set out to find one.

"I am so rich, I can choose whoever I want," he told his dog. "They will be queuing up to marry me."

One day the old squire was admiring his fields of golden corn, when he spotted the farmer's daughter.

"Ho-ho!" he exclaimed. "I can see a wife to be. So young! So strong!" Then his eyes narrowed with greed, "And she will save me money when she's my wife because I won't have to pay her to work." So he invited the girl to his mansion that afternoon.

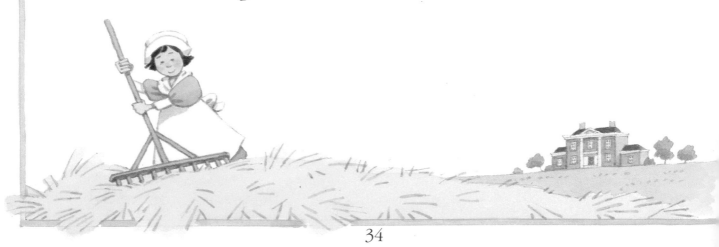

When she arrived he said pompously, "I have news for you. I have decided to get married, and I have chosen you to be my wife."

"Have you now?" said the farmer's daughter. "Well I've got news for you an' all, I don't want to get wed. And even if I did, you'd be the last person *I'd* choose."

The squire couldn't believe his ears. "But ... but ... you must be joking!" he said.

"Do you see me laughing?" she replied. "My answer is 'no', and it will stay 'no' until cows lay eggs and pigs fly!" Before he could say another word, she jumped up and marched out of the house.

The squire's face grew bright red and, stamping his foot with rage, he sent for the farmer.

"That girl of yours is as stubborn as a lazy old donkey!" he roared. "I'll tell you what: if you can get her to marry me, I'll never charge you another rent." Then the squire pointed out of the window. "And what's more, you can have that meadow, the one full of poppies and daisies."

Now the farmer had wanted that meadow for many a long year - and no more rent either! So he said, "Well, sir, that foolish daughter of mine has never known what's best for her. Maybe if we put our heads together, we could come up with a plan that would please everybody."

So that is what they did, and this was the plan they made. The squire would arrange the wedding, with guests, cake and a beautiful dress at the ready. Then, on the wedding day, the farmer would tell his daughter that she was wanted for work at the big house. They were sure that when she arrived and saw everyone assembled for the wedding, she would be too afraid to say "no".

Some weeks later, on the wedding day, the squire called his stable boy and ordered, "Go quickly to the farmer and fetch what he has promised me."

Off ran the stable boy, and meeting the farmer on the road said, "Please, sir, I've come to fetch what you promised the squire."

"Oh, aye," replied the farmer with a smile. "She's down in the meadow."

The stable boy ran off again and soon arrived at the meadow where the farmer's daughter was busy raking hay.

"Miss," he panted, "I've come to fetch what your father promised the squire."

The girl realized at once what the two old men were up to. So, pointing at the old grey mare nibbling the grass nearby, she said, "There she is, take her."

The stable boy leapt on to the mare and galloped back to the squire's mansion as fast as possible - which wasn't very fast as the mare was very old. Then he called up to the squire's window, "Excuse me, your squireship, I've brought her. She's down here."

"Well done," said the squire, thinking the boy had brought the farmer's daughter. "Take her upstairs to my mother's old room."

"But, sir ..." cried the stable boy.

"No buts, boy. Just do as I say, at once!" bellowed the squire.

It wasn't at all easy persuading the mare to climb the stairs. The stable boy pushed and groaned, and the other servants shoved and grunted. This went on for over an hour, until at last, they succeeded in getting her into the bedroom.

"We've done it!" called the stable boy. "Isn't she stubborn!"

"Oh yes, she certainly is," replied the squire. "Now, quickly fetch the maids and dress her in the wedding gown, there's no time to lose."

The stable boy could hardly believe his ears, but he carried out the squire's orders all the same. The maids shrieked and giggled as they tugged at the dress to pull it over the mare's bottom. Finally, they set the wedding veil between her ears.

"She's ready!" called the boy again.

"Well, bring her downstairs, open the door and announce the bride to all my guests," replied the squire, checking his hair in a mirror.

"OK, sir," said the boy. With lots of bumps and thumps, the old grey mare was brought downstairs. The boy threw open the front door and all the guests who were gathered in the garden turned to view the squire's bride. There stood the mare with her veil all crooked, munching the bridal bouquet.

After a few seconds of stunned silence, the guests, the maids and the stable boy began to laugh loudly. This frightened the poor old mare so much that she galloped off back to the peace and quiet of her meadow. As for the squire, he was so taken aback that he sat down on his hat, and squashed it flat.

In a far-off field the farmer's daughter sang as she worked. As she sang she thought about her future, which featured no squires at all.

# THE KING AND HIS THREE CHILDREN

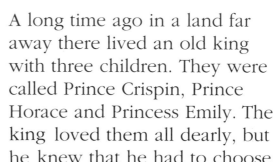

A long time ago in a land far away there lived an old king with three children. They were called Prince Crispin, Prince Horace and Princess Emily. The king loved them all dearly, but he knew that he had to choose one to be the next king or queen. As he got older, the king worried about this more and more. It kept him awake at night. "Who would make the best ruler?" he'd ask his teddy bear.

Then one morning he woke up with an idea. He called his children into his throne room, and said, "Now you know that I love you all." They nodded. "But I can only choose one of you to rule when I die. So I am going to give you a test." He reached into his pocket. "Here is a gold coin for each of you. Whoever can use it to fill the palace from top to bottom will be the next king or queen."

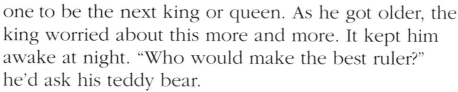

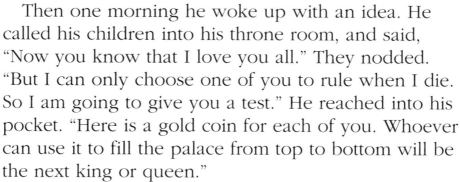

Although this worried the royal children, as the palace had seventy-five rooms and miles of passages, they decided the test was a fair one. So each set off in search of something that would fill it.

Prince Crispin went to sit in the palace garden to ponder. On a tree nearby, he saw a bird building its nest with twigs and feathers.

"That's it!" he cried. "Feathers! With my gold coin I could buy millions of feathers, they'll easily fill the palace." So off he went to see the man who made feather beds.

"How many feathers would you sell me for this gold coin?" asked Prince Crispin.

The feather-bed man's eyes grew wide at the sight of the gold. "Five wagon-loads," he replied.

"Agreed!" said Prince Crispin. And soon he was riding back to the palace with five wagons and a big smile.

Prince Horace went to the market. He looked around at the rolls of cloth, jars of jam and strings of onions. "Oh dear," he sighed. "One gold coin won't buy enough of these things to fill the palace."

He was just about to give up when he heard the sound of a shepherd boy playing a flute. An idea struck him at once.

"Will you sell me your flute for a gold coin?" said Prince Horace to the shepherd boy.

"You bet!" came the reply. So the prince handed over the coin, and all the way home he played a happy tune on his new flute.

Princess Emily spent all day searching the town for something to buy. "It's no good," she said. "The palace is just too big. I shall just have to tell Father that I have failed."

Then, as she turned the corner, her eye was caught by a glimmer of light from a small shop. She looked in at the window and saw the shopkeeper lighting candles and putting them in lanterns.

"Of course!" exclaimed the princess. She rushed into the shop and bought as many candles as she could. Then she ran back to the palace with her bundle, more pleased than a flea on a shaggy dog.

That evening, in the throne room, the king said to his three children, "Show me what you have bought, then I can choose who will succeed me."

Prince Crispin brought in his feathers, which flew everywhere, and made everyone sneeze. When they had settled they only filled twenty rooms of the palace.

"Well done, a good try," said the king.

"Oh flummocks!" said Prince Crispin.

Prince Horace took out the flute he'd bought. He put it to his lips and began to play a tune. When he had finished everyone looked very puzzled.

"Don't you see," said the prince, "I've filled the palace with music."

"Brilliant!" said the king. "No one will beat that."

"Just a moment, Father," said Princess Emily. "Hadn't we better check that the music reached the cellar and the attic?"

"Quite right," said the king, despatching two servants to the topmost and bottommost parts of the palace. "Now then, Horace, play again." His son played an even louder tune.

After a while the servants came back. "When are you going to start?" they said.

Prince Crispin grinned, "They haven't heard the music, so it hasn't filled the whole palace."

"Oh flummocks!" said Prince Horace.

So now it was the turn of Princess Emily. Everyone laughed when they saw her small bundle.

She opened it and sent the servants off to put candles into lanterns all over the palace.

"Make sure you put a lantern in every room," she ordered. "And don't forget the cellar and attic." Then she went round and lit every candle herself.

"There you are, Father," said the princess. "I've filled the whole palace ... with light."

The king was delighted and hugged his daughter. "You are the winner, three cheers for the future queen!"

"Oh double flummocks!" said her brothers.

Princess Emily became a good queen and her people were very happy. Every year after that, to celebrate her birthday, candles were lit in every house. This meant that, not just the palace, but the whole land was filled with light.

# THE WIND
# AND THE SUN

The wind had been cross all week. Huffing and puffing, he had blown down trees, stamped on fields of corn, and sent the chimney on top of Mrs Crabtree's cottage crashing into her garden, just missing her cat.

He was in such a grumpy mood that he began to pick a quarrel with the sun. "I am much stronger than you," he boasted. "You can't blow down trees or nearly flatten a cat like I can. I could even blow clouds in front of you and blot out your sunshine. I am more powerful than anything else in the whole world."

The sun smiled at the wind and replied in a gentle voice, "I know you can do all that, but it doesn't mean that you are more powerful than I am."

"Of course it does, fire-face," roared the wind, blowing a sudden blast at some pigs which almost straightened their tails.

"Let's have a contest to see who's the strongest."

"All right," said the sun. "You see that man walking along the road. Well, I challenge you to see which of us can get his coat off."

"Ha!" puffed the wind with a gust of laughter. "I can do that before you can say 'Easy, peasy, brisk and breezy.'"

"We shall see," said the sun. "You can go first."

The wind took a deep, deep breath. Then he puffed out his cheeks and began to blow a terrific gale. He picked and plucked at the man's coat to try to get it off. It didn't work though, because the more the wind blew, the more the man tightened his belt and wrapped his coat around him.

The wind roared and whooshed with all his might; it was almost a hurricane. Once he even swept the man right off his feet.

The wind blew until he was blue in the face. Eventually he turned to the sun and whispered hoarsely, "I give up ... it's your turn now."

The sun gave a big, broad smile and shone down on the man as brightly as he could. Soon, the poor man had to stop and mop his forehead with a big spotted handkerchief.

"Any minute now," said the sun, sending down a burst of super-scorching sunshine. Sure enough, before the man had gone another thirty paces, he stopped and put down his suitcase again. Then he squinted up at the sun, puffed out his cheeks ... and took off his coat.

"Hooray!" cheered the sun, beaming. "Look at that, I've done it!"

The wind wheezed in his anger, for he now knew that he wasn't the most powerful in the world. Still out of breath, all he could manage to say was, "Oh blow!"

# THE THREE WISHES

Max was a poor woodcutter who lived in a small cottage next to a large forest with his wife, Elsa.

One day, just as he was about to chop down a giant oak tree, he saw a woodland fairy fluttering just below a branch. He had never seen a fairy before. "Maybe I'm dreaming," he said to himself, rubbing his eyes; but when he opened them again, the fairy was still there.

"Hello!" said the tiny creature. "If you spare this oak tree, the next three wishes that you or your wife make will come true." Then she was gone. So Max left the oak tree and moved on to another.

He worked hard all day, and when he got home he was so tired that he had forgotten all about the fairy and the three wishes.

"I'm hungry. What's for supper?" he asked.

"Potato soup," answered Elsa. "We haven't got enough money to buy meat."

"Not again," moaned Max. "I'll begin to look like a potato soon. I wish we could have a nice sausage for a change." No sooner had he spoken when there was a "Tring!", and a huge sausage appeared on the table. This reminded Max of the fairy, and he immediately told Elsa about their three wishes. When he'd finished, Elsa was furious.

"You stupid man, you've wasted one of our precious wishes on a sausage! I wish it was stuck to the end of your nose."

Immediately there was another "Tring!", and the sausage flew from the table and attached itself to the end of Max's nose.

When he next spoke, it sounded as though he had a terrible cold. "Dow look what you've done," he mumbled. "Try and pull it off." Elsa tried, but the sausage was well and truly stuck on.

At last she said, "Let's ask for all the gold and jewels in the world. Then we could enjoy ourselves."

"Don't be silly. How could I enjoy byself wid everybody calling be sausage-dose?" replied Max. "Oh, I wish dis had dever happened."

"Tring!" The sausage disappeared, and so did their third and final wish. They sat down to their potato soup, and argued about whose fault it was. If only they had eaten the sausage when it had first appeared, they would still have had two wishes left.

If you had three wishes, what would you wish for?

# THE NIGHTINGALE

In the days before cars, computers and corn flakes, there lived an emperor called Choo Ning. He was the Emperor of China - a very powerful man. The emperor's palace was the biggest and best in the world. It had the most beautiful gardens, which were so big that Choo Ning hadn't even seen most of them. They stretched for miles: over fields to a lake, and then on to a forest in which lived a nightingale. Beyond the forest was the sea. At night the fishermen would drift past, silently casting their nets and praying for a good catch. As they did so, they would hear the nightingale singing. To them it was a sign that their prayers had been heard.

Important travellers from many countries visited the emperor in his palace. When they returned home they would talk about their adventures, and always they remembered the nightingale and her beautiful song.

One day, a book arrived from the Queen of France. She had visited China the previous summer and had written about her travels. Choo Ning read the book with great pleasure, until he came to these words: "The Emperor of China has many amazing things, but the most amazing of all is the nightingale."

The emperor had never heard of a nightingale.

He summoned his chief adviser, and asked, "What's a nightingale? It's supposed to be the best thing I have, but I haven't a clue what it is. Find out or else I'll have you clean out the royal guinea pigs for a year."

The chief adviser scuttled through the palace asking everyone what a nightingale was. No one knew.

Eventually he came to the kitchen, where a young maid was stirring the soup for supper that night.

"A nightingale?" she said. "It's a bird, of course. It sings every night in the forest."

"Go and fetch it straight away!" commanded the chief adviser.

"Only if you stir this soup," said the girl. "And say please." The chief adviser was so desperate that he did as she asked.

The girl ran to the forest, and soon found the tree in which the nightingale was already singing. "Excuse me, Nightingale, will you come to the palace and sing for the emperor, please?"

"All right," said the nightingale.

Later that evening, the emperor sat at his golden banquetting table facing a golden perch, on which the nightingale had been placed. The emperor nodded, and the nightingale began to sing. She sang many tunes; each was so beautiful, that the emperor soon had tears of joy running down his cheeks, which made his beard all soggy.

"I shall keep you here in a cage," said the emperor when the bird had finished. "Then you can sing for me every day."

"But Emperor," replied the nightingale. "I sing songs of freedom."

"Don't worry, it will be a golden cage, the most valuable in China, if not the world."

Then the nightingale pleaded, "You can't tell the worth of something by what it looks like. What's inside is far more important. How can I build my nest if I am in a cage, even if it is made of gold?"

But the emperor's mind was made up, and the bird was put in the cage. Every evening she sang for Choo Ning.

Some weeks later a parcel arrived for the emperor. On it was a label: "To Choo Ning, I really enjoyed my visit. I loved hearing your nightingale, but how does this one compare with yours? Best wishes from the Emperor of Japan."

He opened the parcel and found a beautiful nightingale made of silver and gold, and studded with

precious jewels. On the side was a key. It was a
clockwork nightingale, and when it was wound up it
sang a beautiful song.

"Fetch the real bird. We'll see which sings the best,"
said the emperor. The nightingale was brought and
both birds sang. Then the emperor said, "Hmm, I
suppose the old bird can sing more tunes, but it looks
extremely shabby. Look how the new bird glitters and
sparkles."

Now everyone wanted to marvel at the clockwork
nightingale, and to hear its one song. The chief
adviser had to wind up the bird fifty times. And fifty
times the bird sang the same tune.

"Now let's hear the scruffy old nightingale again,"
said the emperor. But when they looked in the
golden cage, it was empty. In the excitement, the
door had come unfastened, and the nightingale had
flown away. "Of all the cheek!" said the emperor.
"That bird shall never be allowed in the palace again."

For a year, the emperor listened to the clockwork
nightingale as often as he could. Every visitor
marvelled at the splendour of the jewelled bird and its
wonderful song. But one day, whilst it was singing for
the Queen of Siam, there was a "whirrrr, clunk!" - and
the bird stopped singing.

The royal clockmaker was called. She examined the inside of the bird, then shook her head and said, "Your Excellency, these clockwork parts are very worn. I've done what I can, but the bird should only be made to sing once a day."

Choo Ning became very sad. The only time he ever smiled was when the clockwork nightingale sang its one and only song each day, and even then he wished it could sing other tunes as well.

Several years passed and the emperor lay ill in bed close to death. He opened his eyes from time to time to look at the silver and gold bird. "Please sing for me," he pleaded. But the bird had long since broken and just looked at him dumbly. Then, through the window he heard a song: a strange, yet familiar song. He turned his head and saw the real nightingale land on his window sill.

The bird had answered the emperor's plea, and once more sang tunes that he had not heard for many years. Eventually Choo Ning sighed deeply and closed his eyes.

When he awoke the nightingale was still there.

"You have saved my life," he said. "Will you always come if I promise to let you return to your forest?"

"Yes I will," replied the nightingale. "But only if you also promise to tell no one about me. This way I will be left in peace."

The emperor nodded. "Very well," he said.

"Then I will come," continued the bird. "And I will sing about places and things you cannot see from your palace. My songs will make you a great ruler. I have already shown you one of the most important things you can know: that you cannot tell a person's worth by what's on the outside."

Choo Ning looked back at his old clockwork nightingale, and as he did so one of its wings fell off and fell to the floor with a jangling crash. He smiled, and nodded again.

So the emperor got out of bed, much to everyone's surprise. He lived many more years, and with the help of the nightingale became one of the wisest and kindest emperors China ever had.

# CLEVER MILLIE

 On top of a small, high hill lived
a woman called Millie Smith and
her husband. He was an
enormous man, with muscles as
strong as iron. No one knew his
first name. He was just known as
Big Smithy.

There were two problems with the Smiths' house.
Firstly it faced north, so there was always a cold wind
whistling in through the doors and windows, even in
the summer. Secondly, their well was at the bottom of
the hill, and it was such a struggle for Millie to carry
the full bucket back up again.

Big Smithy was a lazy man. He made his wife do
all the work whilst he boasted about his strength.
"I'm the strongest person in the whole land," he'd say.
Then to prove it he'd throw a rock six fields across
the valley. "My strength can beat anything."

"Brains are better," said Millie, the cleverer of the
two.

"Well you can't be very clever if you think that,"
said Big Smithy, and laughed at the thought that he
had outwitted his wife. But the next week,
Millie Smith got the chance to prove her point.

It was Friday lunchtime when Millie arrived home from town with the week's shopping.

"Are you sure you're the strongest in the land?" she asked Big Smithy, who was busy reading the paper.

"Of course I am," he boomed. "Why?"

"Well, there was a man in town who said that *he* was," came the reply.

Big Smithy stopped reading, and suddenly looked very worried. "Was he over seven feet tall with red hair, a red beard, staring eyes and fists the size of water melons?" he said.

His wife thought for a bit. "Yes, that's him. He called himself ... er, now what was it?"

"Boris," said Big Smithy quietly, his eyes wide and staring.

"Yes, that's it. Do you know him?"

"Know him?" yelled Big Smithy. "I'm afraid I've been lying to you all this time. I'm not the strongest in the land, he is. Only he's been in the south for years, I never thought he'd come up this way." He stopped and thought for a minute. "Maybe he's just up for the day. Yes, that's it, he'll be on his way home by now."

"'Fraid not," said Millie, looking out of the window. "He's coming across the valley towards the house, look!"

Big Smithy screamed, jumped up and ran around the room wildly. "He'll pummel me, he'll bash me, he'll ... mangle-ize me! What am I going to do?"

"Well..." said his wife.

"Millie, you haven't got an idea, have you?"

"What'll you do if I help you?" she said.

"Anything, I'll do anything," he replied, going whiter than a polar bear in a snowstorm.

"Right," she said, squeezing him into a small cot in the corner. "Now stay there, don't say a word and hold this," and she handed him a big rock.

Ten long minutes passed. Then they heard a knock at the door, so loud that it rattled all the windows. Millie Smith opened it and there stood the enormous figure of Boris. He was even bigger than she remembered.

"Where's Big Smithy?" he said, spitting out the words like grape pips.

"He's not in," said Millie. "He's away in the south. He said he was going down there to find a man called Boris. Then he said he was going to bash him to bits and squash him to a jelly."

"What!" said the man. "I am Boris!"

"Oh, that's funny," said Millie, looking him up and down. "He said you were big and strong."

Boris snorted with anger. "I am big and strong. I'm bigger and stronger than he is."

"Then you'll be able to do anything he can do."

"And more," said Boris. "I am Boris the Brave! I am Boris the Brilliant! I am Boris the, er ..." but he couldn't think of anything else beginning with B.

Millie wondered why so many men spent so much time boasting about how great they were. Then she said, "Every day, Big Smithy turns the house round to the south so it gets the sun."

"That's a child's job," said Boris, taking off his jacket, which could have doubled as a tent. He put his shoulder against the house, and heaved and huffed. With a huge scraping and rumbling, the house was slowly turned right around. Millie blinked into the sunshine, and breathed in the nice warm breeze.

"There," said Boris. "What else can he do?"

"Big Smithy's so strong, he could take a long stick and drive it right through the hill," said the clever woman.

"Baby's job!" said Boris, and he went and fetched a log that was as tall as the house. Then he raised it above his head, and with a huge shout he drove it downwards so hard that it disappeared completely into the hill.

"There!" he said triumphantly. Millie looked into the hole, and dropped in a small pebble. There was a moment's silence, then ... "splash", the pebble had hit some water. She now had a well at the top of the hill.

"Now you'd better go down south and fight Big Smithy," said Millie.

Boris was quite tired, although he didn't say so. "I think I'll have some bread before I go," he said, and pushed his way into the house. It was then that he saw Big Smithy in the cot.

"Big Smithy!" he snarled, and strode across the room towards him. Smithy was so scared that he started to shake. He clenched his fist so hard around the rock Millie had given him, that it shattered into a million pieces.

Just before Boris reached the cot, Millie shouted,

66

"Watch out Boris, that's Baby Smithy. If you harm him, Big Smithy won't be very pleased."

Boris stopped. "*Baby* Smithy?" he said, looking at the size of the person in the cot. Then he glanced down at the crushed rock on the floor and suddenly felt very weak. He rushed out of the door, down the hill and was never seen around those parts again.

Big Smithy was so scared that he shook for three days afterwards. He was true to his word, though, and eventually he said, "You were right, Millie Smith: brains are best. I suppose you'll want me to do all the jobs around the house now."

"No," said Millie. "Just do half of them ... and stop boasting." And so the two of them lived happily for the rest of their days.

# THE LONELY GIANT

Bigg, the giant, was always playing tricks on people. Sometimes he would stamp on the ground to make an earthquake. At other times he would cough to make a sound like thunder. His favourite trick, though, was to disguise his nose as a hill. Then as people climbed up to the top, he'd sneeze and tumble them all down again. He always laughed when his tricks worked, but deep down Bigg was very unhappy; he was a lonely giant.

One day, he saw an old woman walking through the wood. He decided to do his thunder-cough so she would think it was about to rain; but rather than run home to take in her washing, she turned on him.

"So, you thought you could give me a fright, eh? Well, I don't want one, thank you." Bigg was taken aback. After all, she was so small and he was so ... well, big. "I can give you something that *you* want, though," she said. "Happiness. I bet I can make you happy within a day."

"What do you bet?" asked Bigg, who was becoming very interested.

"If I make you happy, you must promise never to play another trick on anyone," answered the old woman.

"What if you don't make me happy?" he said.

"Then I will be your servant for ever."

Bigg could never resist a challenge, especially one he was sure to win. Because even if by some chance she did make him happy, he wouldn't admit it. So he said, "All right!"

"Good, let's have a drink to settle it," said the old woman, handing Bigg a bottle.

"What have I got to lose?" said Bigg, gulping down the liquid in one swallow. However, no sooner had he finished, than there was a large flash. Bigg started to feel his head spin. Then he started to shrink. He got smaller and smaller until he was staring up at the old woman. In fact he was child-sized.

"You tricked me!" he said.

"Don't worry. The magic only lasts for a day," replied the woman. "After that you will turn back into a giant again." Then she turned and walked away.

Bigg walked into the town. When he was a giant it only used to take him ten strides, but now it took ten minutes. With each step he got more and more sulky and miserable.

In the town he recognized some children he had scared the week before. "I'll shake them up a bit," thought Bigg.

Forgetting he was now the same size as them, he stamped on the ground to make them think it was an earthquake. But as he was small, nothing happened and the children just looked at him in amazement.

"Look at that boy. He's doing a dance," said one.

They all loved dancing, so they immediately joined in, jumping and stamping next to Bigg.

# THE GOLDEN WINDOWS

Mary was a young girl who lived with her mother in a house on the side of a valley. From her garden she could look across the valley to another house. It was a very special one because it had golden windows.

Mary had always longed to visit this house. As she played in the garden she would often stop and gaze at the beautiful windows shimmering like flames in the afternoon sun. Then she would sigh and say to herself, "I wish I could live in a house like that. It must be wonderful to look out through golden windows."

Sometimes she would ask her mother to take her across the valley for a walk. But her mother would say, "Not today, Mary, I've got so much to do. Maybe another day, when I'm not so busy."

For her seventh birthday, Mary's grandmother gave her a shiny new bicycle. Mary was thrilled, and it wasn't long before she was an expert rider. As there wasn't much traffic along the lane next to her house, Mary was allowed to go for short rides on her own. Then one day, she had an idea.

"Mummy," she asked. "Please may I ride across the valley? I'd really love to go and see the house with golden windows."

Mary's mother knew that Mary rode her bike very sensibly, so she said, "All right, but do be careful, and ..."

"Thanks!" said Mary, rushing out of the house.

"And be back in time for tea!" shouted her mother after her.

Mary set off, keeping very close to the side of the road, and going round each bend with great care. As she got closer to the house, she became more and more excited. At last she would be able to see the golden windows close up. Maybe, if she was really lucky, the people who lived in the house would let her touch them.

Eventually she reached the front gate of the house. She propped her bicycle against the hedge and lifted the latch. "I'll wait until I'm in the garden before I look," she thought, holding her breath with anticipation. "I can hardly wait."

However, as she opened the gate, she could contain herself no longer. She must look at those beautiful golden windows. But as she raised her head, her heart sank; her tingle of excitement turned to an ache of disappointment.

"But they're glass, just plain old glass," she said softly, near to tears. "They're ... they're just ... ordinary. And all the time I thought they were made of gold."

She didn't bother to go any further. She closed the gate, picked up her bicycle, and turned it around ready for the long ride home. As she set off, she glanced across the valley and saw something which made her stop. She could see her own house - and the windows were gold! They were blazing like golden flames. Then she realized why: they too were reflecting the rays of the afternoon sun. So she did live in a house with golden windows after all.

# THE MILLER, HIS SON AND THEIR DONKEY

One day, a miller and his son were taking their donkey to sell at a market in a neighbouring town. On the way they met a group of young girls. "Look!" said one of them, pointing. "Fancy trudging along this dusty road when one of them could be riding on the donkey. How silly!"

The miller was a kind man, so he said to his son, "That's a good idea. You have a ride. Up you get." And he helped his son on to the donkey.

They carried on with their journey, and after a while, they came across three old men. "Hey, miller!" shouted one. "That son of yours is a real lazy-bones. He's the one who should be walking, not you."

"Hmm, perhaps they are right," said the miller, and changed places with his son.

They travelled a bit further, and then they met a small crowd of women and children. One of the women pointed at them and said, "You selfish old man! Why don't you let the poor boy ride, too?"

"She's got a point, there," said the miller, and he lifted up his son. They carried on with their journey, both riding the donkey.

They had almost reached the town, when a man coming the other way asked, "Is that your donkey?"

"Yes it is," answered the miller. "We're taking him to sell at the market. Why do you ask?"

"Well, the poor old beast will soon be worn out, carrying you two," said the man, stroking the donkey's nose. "Who'll want to buy him then? Surely it would be much better if you carried the donkey."

The miller and his son looked at each other.

"That's a very good idea," said the miller, and with the help of a strong pole and some rope, they carried the donkey into town.

The people of the town had never seen anything so funny before.

"Just look at that!" said one man. "They're trying to carry a donkey!" They all laughed until tears rolled down their cheeks.

Now, the donkey didn't mind being carried, but he hated being laughed at. So he kicked and struggled at the rope until it broke with a "Snap!". Then he galloped out of the town and was never seen again.

The miller and his son walked sadly home. "I shouldn't have tried to please so many people," he said with a sigh. "I ended up pleasing no one. It looks like I'm the donkey now."

# PRINCESS TABATHA'S NEW TRICK

King Theodore and Queen Phoebe were much loved by everyone in the land. However, the same could not be said of their daughter, Princess Tabatha. She was what might be called a royal little beast.

Tabatha loved to play tricks on people. Her best ones were: putting mouldy yoghurt on the underside of door handles so that the servants kept getting their hands messy, and creeping up on the cook's cat when it was asleep, then barking loudly like a dog which made it yowl with fright. Her favourite, though, was to raise the drawbridge just as the royal limousine was arriving at the palace. She loved to see it screech to a halt in front of the moat.

She would have put big spiders into the beds of important visitors, but for the fact that she was scared stiff of spiders.

One day, Princess Tabatha was in her private bathroom. The queen thought she was brushing her teeth, but really she was making water bombs to drop from the window on to the castle sentries. She filled the last bag with water, then went to unlock the door. The key was stuck. She tugged harder, and eventually it turned, but Tabatha had had an idea. The water bombs were forgotten in a splash.

Tabatha locked the door again, then started to cry loudly, "Help, I'm stuck in the bathroom! He-e-e-elp!" The cook heard the screams, left her baking and rushed up the stairs. She tried hard to open the door, while inside Princess Tabatha just sat on the edge of the bath and read a comic.

After ten minutes, Tabatha turned the key, opened the door and said with a mischievous smile, "Oh dear, silly me forgot to unlock it."

The cook was about to tell her off, when the smoke alarm went off in the kitchen. "My cakes!" she cried, and rushed downstairs.

On Saturday, when she knew that a servant was in the middle of loading the washing machine, Princess Tabatha tried the same trick. "Help, I'm stuck in the bathroom! He-e-elp!" It worked again. As the servant rushed up the stairs, she opened the door and said, "That made you run!"

He was so cross that he put too much powder in the washing machine, which made it overflow with bubbles.

That evening the king and queen had to go to a very important state banquet. Shirley, the babysitter, was watching her favourite detective series on the television when she heard, "Help, I'm stuck in the bathroom! He-e-elp!"

"Coming!" shouted Shirley. Then she jumped up and ran upstairs as fast as she could.

She was met by a smiling Princess Tabatha who said, "That had you worried!"

Shirley said crossly, "One day you'll try that trick and no one will believe you!" This woke the young princes, who started screaming, so Shirley had to quieten them down. By the time she went back to the television, she'd missed the end of the show.

Over the next few days the naughty princess tried her new trick on just about everyone. Then on Wednesday evening her parents were enjoying an evening off, when there came a huge scream.

"Mummy! Daddy! I'm stuck in the bathroom with a massive spider! He-e-elp!" The king and queen knew how scared she was of spiders. They rushed to the bathroom, but try as they might, they could not open the door. Inside, Tabatha carried on crying.

"She must be telling the truth," said the queen.

"I'm going to call a fire engine," said the king.

Soon, a wailing siren could be heard in the castle courtyard. The fire officers rushed in and started attacking the door with their axes. They broke it down, only to find Tabatha sitting in the bath reading a book.

"Where's the fire?" she said, with a grin. The king went as red as a fire engine, and apologized profusely.

One night during the following week, after the shattered bathroom door had been repaired, Princess Tabatha went to her bathroom to get a drink of water. The door, being new, was a bit stiff, and as she went to leave, she found it stuck. She tugged and pulled as hard as she could for ages, but with no success. The door was stuck fast, really stuck.

She sat down on the edge of the bath. She'd just started to think how she could turn this into her best trick yet, when her eyes rested on something which made her blood run cold. Crawling out of the plug-hole in the bath was the biggest, blackest, hairiest spider she'd ever seen. She leapt across the room and pressed herself against the wall, staring at the spider, which was now on the edge of the bath. It really was a monster.

For a full minute she was too terrified to shout, but

when she did it was very loud. "AAGHH! SPIDER! HELP! I'M STUCK! AAAGGHH!"

Soon she heard the king's voice outside the door. "Sorry Tabatha, you've tried that trick once too often - we're not falling for it again. You can come out whenever you want to. Goodnight." And he went back to bed.

Tabatha spent the worst night of her life. Although the spider went to sleep on the edge of the bath, Tabatha thought it was wide awake and ready to pounce. So she stood, rigid, glued to the wall, her eyes fixed on the spider all night.

In the morning, the spider had just disappeared back down the plug hole when her father pushed open the door to discover his white-faced daughter. "No harm done," he said, looking into the empty bath. "You'd better get to bed now."

Princess Tabatha was too tired to protest. She got into bed, and soon went to sleep; but she woke up a completely different girl.

# SILLY MCADAM

Not too long ago there lived a man called Adam McAdam. His wife called him something different. She worked very hard, but Adam McAdam always seemed to lose their money; so she called him Silly McAdam.

"You drive me round the bend!" she'd often scream, which is what some people say when they are at their wits' end.

Now you might think Mrs McAdam was a bit of a nag; but she wasn't. She was just an extremely nice woman, married to an extremely silly man.

One morning, after a week in which Adam McAdam had been especially silly, his wife was counting their money. It didn't take her very long. "Two buttons and an old bus ticket. We're broke thanks to you," she said. "You drive me round the bend!"

"Sorry," he replied.

"We've not even enough to buy a piece of pizza. There's nothing for it, you'll have to go to an old junk sale. There's one in town this afternoon. Come on, we'll look out some old stuff - we must have something that people will want to buy."

They both hunted in the attic, searched in the cellar, and grubbed around in the garage. At the end

of the morning, they looked at the pile of assorted junk. There was a tennis racket with three strings, a jigsaw with some pieces missing, a lamp in the shape of a ship, an old wooden toilet seat and lots more not-very-useful things.

"This lot should fetch something," said Mrs McAdam. "Though it's a pity we haven't got one decent thing to sell."

After they had loaded up the car, Adam McAdam fetched the old leather flying helmet and goggles which he always wore for driving. (As he drove along, he liked to pretend he was flying an aeroplane, and he used the horn to shoot down enemy planes.)

"Of course! Why didn't I think of it before?" said Mrs McAdam. "You can sell that silly old helmet. It's pretty old, so it's sure to fetch quite a bit."

"Oh, but it's my favourite thing ..." complained Adam; but he stopped when he saw the look on his wife's face. "I'll sell it," he sighed.

Adam McAdam drove the car down the road towards the town. As he bumped along (the car was very old) he saw his friend Wally walking along in the same direction. He slowed down and stopped next to him.

"Hello Wally, do you want a lift?"

"No thanks," said Wally, "I'm just looking for somewhere to sit to eat my lunch." At the mention of the word "lunch", Adam McAdam's tummy gave a loud grumble.

"I'll swap you something for your lunch," he said, jumping out and opening the car. There was nothing that Wally wanted, until he noticed the old leather flying helmet on Adam's head.

In a minute, Adam was driving along chewing a peanut butter sandwich, without his flying helmet, which was now Wally's. When he reached the town, he suddenly realized he had no idea where the junk sale was to be held, so he stopped to ask a man. As he pulled over, his wheels bumped on the kerb, and the back door flew open.

The man stopped and looked inside the car.

"I expect you're going to the junk sale," he said.

"Yes, how did you know?" said Adam.

"Oh, just a hunch," replied the man. "Tell you what, I'll give you ten gold coins for the lot." He had worked out that if he were to sell Adam's junk, he'd get much more.

"Ten gold coins?" said Adam.

"All right, eleven, I can't say fairer than that. But you'll have to throw in the car as well."

"OK," said Adam, handing the man the car keys. Adam McAdam was just about to head for home, when a noise made him stop in his tracks. He looked up the road and saw a woman with a one-man band. She was playing to a large crowd who clapped loudly and threw money into her hat.

"That's a good way of making money," thought Adam McAdam. He went up to the woman. "I'll give you eleven gold coins for your band," he said.

"OK," she replied. "I'm far too old for this anyway."

Adam McAdam began to play the one-man band. Very soon he realized there was a problem with his plan: he had never played music before. The noise he made was worse than terrible.

The crowd started to boo at him, and shout rude things such as, "Shut up!" and "Do us a favour!" One woman said, "Sounds like six cats fighting in a dustbin!" Then one by one they all went away covering their ears, leaving Adam McAdam alone. There was nothing for it but to head for home.

It took him ages, as the one-man band was very heavy. He had nearly arrived at his house, when he saw Wally again.

Wally said, "Please help me, Adam. It's my son's birthday tomorrow and I haven't got him a present yet, and now all the shops are closed."

Adam thought, then had a brain wave. "What about this!" he said, pointing to the one-man band.

"Brilliant!" shouted Wally. "Oh, but I haven't any money."

"I'll swap it for my old leather flying helmet," said Adam. And the two men swapped again.

So it was that Adam McAdam arrived home.

"Did you sell the stuff?" asked his wife.

"Er ... yes," he replied.

"Well at least you've done something right. Give me the money, please."

"I swapped it for a one-man band," said Adam.

"Well, give me that, then," said his wife.

"I swapped it with Wally for my old flying helmet," he replied.

"Why did he have your helmet, you silly man?" asked his wife.

"Because I swapped it for his lunch on my way to town," he said again.

Mrs McAdam's eyes grew wide, and she started to shake with rage. "You drive me round the bend!" she said through clenched teeth. "You mean to tell me you left with a load of stuff and a flying helmet, and you've come back with just the helmet?"

"Well ... um ... yes," said Silly Adam.

"Silly McAdam!" she shouted. "You've driven me round the bend for long enough - now I'm going to drive *you* round the bend!"

"But you can't. I sold the car as well."

"Then I'll use this!" she said, picking up a walking stick. She chased him out of the house, and true to her word she drove him right round the bend.

# THE GIVING TREE

Once there was a forest where few people ever went. In the middle of this forest was a clearing in which stood a tree. Its trunk was straight and tall, its branches were strong, its leaves were beautiful and its fruit tasted like heaven.

One morning the tree awoke, as usual, to the chorus of birds and other forest creatures. It stretched its branches and rustled its leaves to greet the new day. Then it looked down and saw a basket in which slept a small baby girl.

The tree waited, but no one came for it. After a while the baby woke up and started to cry.

"You're hungry," said the tree. "You can have my fruit." The tree shook one of its branches. A fruit fell into the baby's mouth and turned immediately into juice sweeter than mother's milk.

Six times during that day the baby cried, and each time the tree fed her with its fruit. The next morning, the basket and the baby had gone.

94

Ten years later, a young girl stood in front of the tree. "Don't you recognize me?" she said. "I was the baby you fed. What will you give me now?"

"You can have my twigs and leaves," said the tree. The girl climbed the tree and played in its branches. She swung on them, used them as a tightrope, then broke off a large twig and made it into a sword for a game of pirates. In the heat of the day, the tree's leaves shaded the girl from the sun. As evening came, the girl left.

Some years later the girl came back. Now she was a teenager. "What will you give me?" she asked.

"You can have my branches," said the tree. So the girl sawed the branches off the tree, and took them away to build herself a wooden house.

More years passed. When the girl came back, she was a young woman. "What will you give me now?"

"You can have my trunk," said the tree.

The girl chopped down the trunk, and from it made a dug-out canoe. Then she took it to the sea and set off on her travels. The tree was now a stump.

Many years passed. Then one day an old woman stood next to the tree stump.

The woman asked, "What will you give me now?"

The tree replied, "I have no more to offer than what I am. You can have my stump."

The old woman sat down. "All these years you have given me food, shelter, play and travel. Now what can I give you, Tree?"

"I was there at your beginning, and now I am the last page in your book. Tell me about your life."

So the old woman told the tree all about her life and travels: the people and places she had seen and been to. The tree listened. As night drew on, the old woman didn't leave. She curled up on the stump and fell asleep for the last time.

That night something magical happened, and next morning, in that clearing in the forest where few people ever went, there stood the tree. It was more beautiful, and wiser than it had ever been.